5/04

D0520584

For Momo

COPYRIGHT © 2003 BY BRUCE INGMAN

ALL RIGHTS RESERVED.

FIRST U.S. EDITION 2003

LIBRARY OF CONGRESS CATALOGING-IN-PUBLICATION
DATA IS AVAILABLE.

LIBRARY OF CONGRESS CATALOG CARD NUMBER 2002073627

ISBN 0-7636-2072-6

10 9 8 7 6 5 4 3 2 1

PRINTED IN ITALY

THIS BOOK WAS TYPESET IN FUTURA.
THE ILLUSTRATIONS WERE DONE IN ACRYLIC.

CANDLEWICK PRESS
2067 MASSACHUSETTS AVENUE
CAMBRIDGE, MASSACHUSETTS 02140

VISIT US AT WWW.CANDLEWICK.COM

TERMS AND CONDITIONS FOR READING THIS BOOK!

1. When you get to the end, say, "Again, please!"
2. Put book under the bed or somewhere safe.
3. No sticky fingers or ripping pages.
4. Lots of giggling.
5. Say please.
6. Look smart.
7. Say thank you!

Boston
← 3,265 miles

Sydney
↓ a long way

Photographs:

Toy Story (page 22) – Walt Disney Co.

King Kong (page 22) – RKO courtesy of The Kobal Collection

Star Wars (page 23) – Lucasfilm Ltd. courtesy of The Kobal Collection

Thanks to Jessica Ingman, Cait Robertson, and Ellie Robertson

BAD NEWS! I'M IN CHARGE!

CANDLEWICK PRESS
CAMBRIDGE, MASSACHUSETTS

Bruce Ingman

Used to be,
my mom would say, Danny!
Clean up!
Tuck your shirt in!
OUTSIDE
NOW!

And take that **THING** with you.

That **THING** was my

fantastic superduper metal detector.

I found all sorts of stuff . . .

The finder of this charter is the new owner and ruler of this land.
By law.

I didn't waste any time . . .

to be some **chang** s around h re!

I appointed my
SPECIAL OPS SQUAD.

I gave them ID cards and the secret password to get them inside S.O.S. headquarters for secret meetings.

I set about ruling

iny land.

List of Changes

1. Stay up late

2. Chips with everything

3. Snacks all the time

4. Every Wednesday teachers wear funny hats

5. Wild parties every week

6. Wear what you like

7. Make your mom + dad wait outside in the car while you visit the toy store for hours & hours

8. Friends around every day

9. No dentists! No hairdressers!

10. ~~No~~ Pets in school

11. Mom + Dad in bed by 8 o'clock

IT'S OFFICIAL!

School
was so much more fun.

straight to my room.

My new rules were very popular.

But sometimes I had to put my

foot down . . .

HOW TO EMBARRASS YOUR KIDS!

Monday

Judge cabbage competition.

Tuesday

Kiss babies.

Wednesday

Launch ship.

Thursday

Judge beauty contest.

Friday

Open toothbrush factory.

Saturday

Attend opera concert.

Sunday

Rest one hour.

Monday

Kiss more

Then one day an unexpected visitor from the

CENTRAL BUREAU

came looking for me. There was more to being in charge than I thought.

Wednesday
Launch ship.

Thursday
Judge beaut[y]
contest.

I couldn't take another
week of this!

with my Cabinet ⟶

Secretary of Being Polite

Secretary of Shaking Hands

Secretary of Carpooling

Secretary of Cleaning

Secretary of Games

⟵ and gave each member

But I kept the best one for myself:

PRESIDENT OF FUN!